# Barbara Reid

# FOX WALKED ALONE

## Scholastic Canada Ltd.

Toronto  New York  London  Auckland  Sydney
Mexico City  New Delhi  Hong Kong  Buenos Aires

Night after night, Fox walked alone,
Came home to a bed made of feathers and bone.
He hunted at night and slept through the day,
Fox walked alone, he liked it that way.

But one day . . .

Fox woke up.
Slipped out of his lair.
Looked. Listened. Sniffed.
There was something in the air.

"That crazy fox!" the ravens said.
"What's he doing out of bed?"

Two mice ran under Fox's nose,
A mole bumped into Fox's toes,
Two tortoises, a pair of hares . . .
Fox was not expecting bears.

A porcupine . . .

and then another.

A wolf asked, "Will you join us, brother?"

"There's something going on," Fox thought.
"I'll take a little walk — why not?
But just in case these strangers bite,
I'll follow safely out of sight."

Fox walked until his paws were sore –
He'd never walked so far before.

"That crazy fox!" the ravens said.
One rolled her eyes, one shook his head.

At last the creatures stopped to rest,
Piling into one big nest.
"Yoo-hoo, Fox!" said Kangaroo,
"Leopard saved a spot for you!"

So tooth and claw and fur and feather,
They all lay down to sleep together.

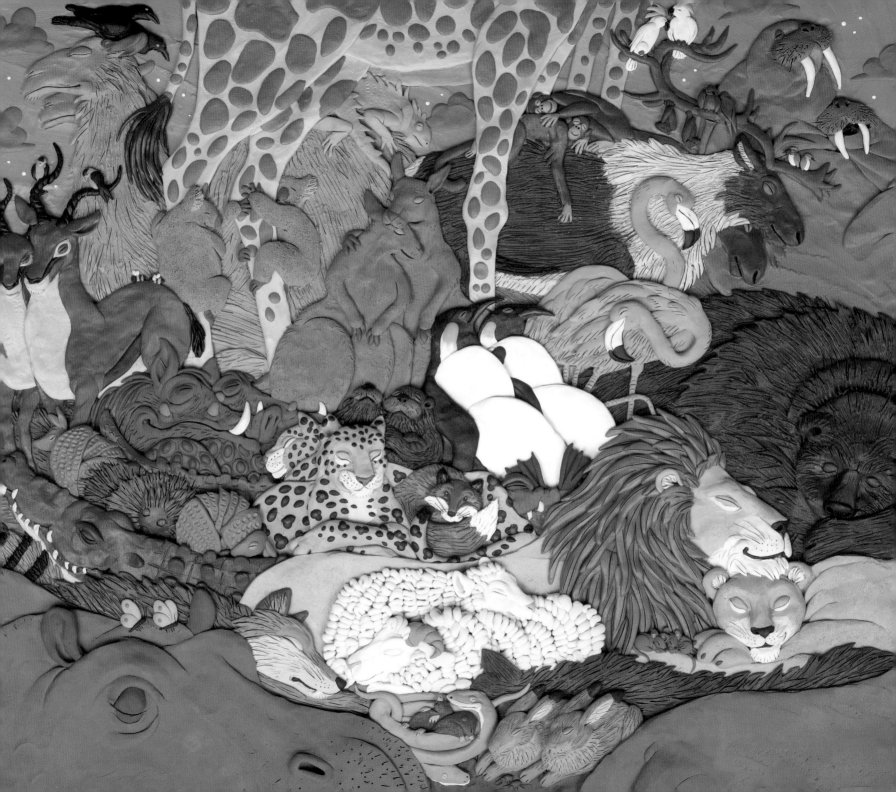

By first light they were on their way –
It wasn't safe, they couldn't stay.
The sky was odd, the wind was wrong . . .
Fox thought he'd better tag along.

And every place they hurried through,
More creatures joined them, two by two.

They crossed a wasteland bare and dead;
A ruined city lay ahead.
Fox wished that he had stayed in bed.
"That crazy fox!" the ravens said.

They picked their way in single file.
Fox figured it would take a while.
He tried to find a bite to eat,
And lost himself in dead-end streets.

He heard a cry. "Did someone call?"
Caught in a cage in a market stall,
Two doves cried, "Fox! It's up to you!
Help us, please! We must come too!"
Fox knew exactly what to do.

He opened the door,

and out they flew.

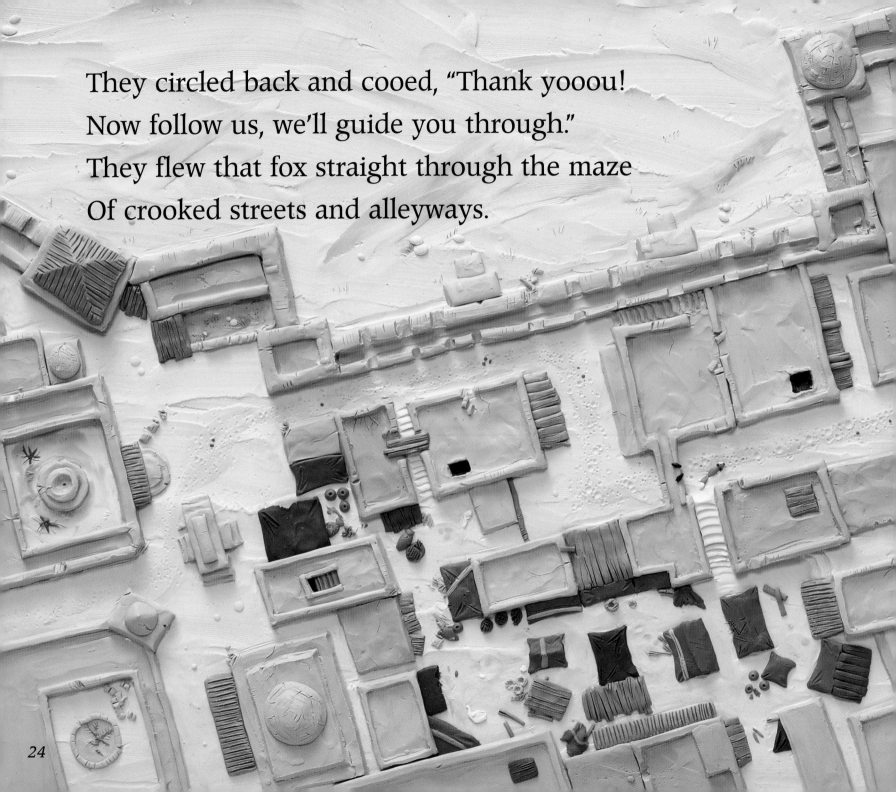

They circled back and cooed, "Thank yooou!
Now follow us, we'll guide you through."
They flew that fox straight through the maze
Of crooked streets and alleyways.

Over a hill, around a bend,
At last he saw their journey's end.
But standing on the dusty plain
Was something Fox could not explain.
"Is this why we have come so far?"

Then someone said, "Oh, there you are!
You're the one I'm waiting for!"
They raced each other to the door.

As Noah welcomed one and all,

A steady rain began to fall.

"That clever fox!" the ravens cried.
Quick as a wink, they flew inside.

*For my teachers*
— B.R.

The illustrations for this book were made with Plasticine that is shaped and pressed onto illustration board.

The text type was set in 20 point Poppl-Pontifex BE.

**Photography by Ian Crysler.**

**Scholastic Canada Ltd.**
604 King Street West, Toronto, Ontario M5V 1E1, Canada

**Scholastic Inc.**
557 Broadway, New York, NY 10012, USA

**Scholastic Australia Pty Limited**
PO Box 579, Gosford, NSW 2250, Australia

**Scholastic New Zealand Limited**
Private Bag 94407, Greenmount, Auckland, New Zealand

**Scholastic Children's Books**
Euston House, 24 Eversholt Street, London NW1 1DB, UK

**Library and Archives Canada Cataloguing in Publication**
Reid, Barbara, 1957-
Fox walked alone / Barbara Reid.

ISBN 978-0-545-98998-5
1. Foxes--Juvenile fiction. I. Title.
PS8585.E4484F69 2009    jC813'.54    C2008-904888-1

ISBN-10 0-545-98998-1

First paperback edition published 2008.

6 5 4 3 2 1        Printed in Singapore        09  10  11  12  13  14